The Summer
Without You

Petar Andonovski was born in 1987, in Kumanovo, north Macedonia. He studied general and comparative literature at the Faculty of Philology, at the University of Cyril and Methodius in Skopje. He has published one poetry collection and five novels. In 2015 his novel *The Body One Must Live In* won the national award for Novel of the Year. *Fear of Barbarians* received the 2020 European Union Prize for Literature. His work has been translated across Europe.

Christina E. Kramer is professor emerita at the University of Toronto. She is the author of numerous articles on the Macedonian language and the Balkans and a translator of Macedonian literature, including *The Fear of Barbarians* by Petar Andonovski; *Freud's Sister* by Goce Smilevski; *My Father's Books, The Time of the Goats* and *The Path of the Eels*, by Luan Starova; *A Spare Life* and *Grandma Non-Oui* by Lidija Dimkovska.

With Support from

The Ministry of Arts of the government
of North Macedonia
Министерство за култура.

The Summer Without You

Petar Andonovski

Translated by

Christina E. Kramer

Parthian, Cardigan SA43 1ED
www.parthianbooks.com
© Petar Adonovski
© Christina E Kramer
This book has been selected to receive financial assistance from English PEN's PEN
Translates programme, supported by Arts Council England. English PEN exists to
promote literature and our understanding of it, to uphold writers' freedoms around the
world, to campaign against the persecution and imprisonment of writers for stating their
views, and to promote the friendly co-operation of writers and the free exchange of ideas.
www.englishpen.org

Published with the support of the Books Council of Wales
Published with support of the Ministry of Culture of the government of North Macedonia
Министерство за култура.

ISBN: 9781914595813
ISBN ebook: 9781917140188
Editor: Gina Harrison
Cover image: Oskar Ulvur, Trevillion Images
Cover design: Syncopated Pandemonium
Typeset by Elaine Sharples
Printed by 4Edge UK
A cataloguing record for this book is available from the British Library

Eros the melter of limbs (now again) stirs me –
sweetbitter unmanageable creature who steals in.

Sappho*

While kissing Agathon, my soul leapt to my
lips...

Plato**

*Translation from Anne Carson, *If Not, Winter: Fragments of Sappho*
p. 130
**Translation from Plato, Loeb Classics, *Diogenes Laertius:*
Lives of Eminent Philosophers 3. Plato p. 305

DISAPPEARANCE

1.

At the beginning of the summer, I had to spend two weeks in hospital. On the last day of my first week, Vlado came and told me I was going to leave early. When we got in the car, he pulled a white envelope from the glove compartment. There were two names on it. His and mine. I still couldn't move my right arm because of the injury. He opened the envelope. He pulled out two airplane tickets and placed them on my knee.

If I hadn't fallen from the balcony, what happened later would likely never have happened at all. Vlado had organised a party to celebrate his twenty-year acting career. I was against this party from the beginning. Vlado hadn't played a single major role in his career. He just got minor, insignificant parts. Once he was offered a role in a movie. During the two-hour running time of the film, he appeared for all of ten seconds. Afterwards, he gathered all his friends to treat them. Vlado loves parties. He takes every opportunity to be with his people. He thrives on their attention. That's probably why he's an actor. I've spent my whole life in a library. First in the reading room and then as a librarian. All I enjoyed was reading books and writing reviews. I was like Vlado's shadow. I went everywhere with him, but no one noticed me. It was the same that evening. In addition to his friends and colleagues, he had invited theatre people and politicians. He's one of those people who gets close to any power. You'd often see members of the opposition parties at his gatherings as well. He figured you should always have good relations with them for when they came to power; it would then be easier to become their favourite. Even though I think that's hypocritical, I've never told him. I had no opinion about anything. Not even the books I wrote reviews about. I only ever published positive reviews, never negative ones. I know that Vlado thinks that's hypocritical, but he's never told me.

That evening Ivan was also at the party. Vlado and I hadn't mentioned him for more than twenty years. Whenever we saw him on television, we'd immediately change the channel. Or whenever one of our friends mentioned him, Vlado would immediately change the subject.

I avoided him all that evening, just as I had all those years. I simply said hello, then left, just like he had twenty years before. With no explanation. I felt bitter that Ivan was there and angry that Vlado hadn't told me he'd been invited.

I found a haven in a dark corner of the balcony. The whole city was spread out below me. I stood next to a willow tree whose branches fell across the city lights. Other than a waiter who came by with a tray of drinks, no one came out to see me. Not even Vlado. I drank alcohol that evening for the first time in a long time. I wanted the party to end as soon as possible. I grabbed anything that came to hand from the tray. I drank quickly until I felt a roiling in my stomach. I turned towards the railing and began to throw up. And then darkness enveloped me. I felt like I was falling onto the city. I felt a strong blow to my head. My right arm tingled. I tried to shift my body, but I couldn't move. A moment later I no longer felt anything.

I awoke in hospital. Luckily for me, there was another, larger balcony on the floor below. Vlado was standing beside me, looking at me with concern. Ivan stood behind him. When I saw him, I closed my eyes. I didn't want him to see me like this. I wanted to say something to him, but I was afraid to open my mouth. I still felt like I was going to vomit. Then I sank again into darkness.

Vlado wanted to give us another chance with a vacation together.

This trip was supposed to bring us closer, so he decided not to invite any friends along with us like he did every other summer.

Then, at the beginning of the summer, several days after I had left the hospital, we set off on our trip. Him and me. Alone. To the island of Crete.

2.

Vlado wanted us to spend as much of our time alone as possible. We didn't go to the small beach that belonged to the hotel. He thought it would be nicer if we spent our time at a wild beach at the edge of the town, far away from anyone else. Vlado rented a car so we wouldn't have to walk there every day. I sensed that he'd been preparing this trip for months. He had planned our every step. Which restaurants we would eat in, what beaches we'd go to, where we'd rent a car. This was not typical of him. Until then, we'd always travelled with his friends, who planned all our trips. He always justified himself by saying that he was too busy, that he wasn't good at organising and that it would be best if his friends planned the trip for us.

Since there was no one else on the wild beach, we didn't need to wear bathing suits. As we lay naked next to one another, the only thing I felt was shame. We had been sleeping in separate beds for ten years. Vlado always gets home too late. Often drunk. He wants to tell me about the many people who had come up and wanted to have their pictures taken with him, how many women and men had chased after him. I pretend to be asleep, but that doesn't stop him from talking. When he comes in, he turns on the lights in the whole apartment. When he comes into the bedroom, he calls out loudly 'gooood eeeevening', and then he tosses his shoes across the room. After he gets undressed, he gets in bed, usually naked, and immediately falls asleep. Then I get up, turn off all the lights, and then can't fall asleep for a long time. The next morning, when I tell him his behaviour bothers me, he just laughs and asks me, 'Is that what I did? and what did I say next?'

That is, until the evening I decided to sleep in the guest room, which we used only when Vlado's parents were visiting. All night I heard him muttering, thinking I was still beside him. The next morning over breakfast, he asked me why I had got up so early. He hadn't even noticed that I hadn't slept beside him. I continued to sleep in the guest room the following nights. And he continued to talk to himself as if I were there beside him. He never asked me why we weren't sleeping in the same bed anymore.

Lying there naked beside him on the beach, I felt extremely uncomfortable. How long had it been since we had lain beside each other. Shame washed over me like when you strip naked in front of someone for the first time when you're going to spend the night with them. I wasn't thinking about passion at all, that simply didn't happen with us. Unlike me, he was calm. He had no problem getting undressed, and he lay down first. When he saw I was still standing there, he looked at me in surprise and said, 'What are you waiting for, take your clothes off and lie down.' I lay down but didn't last there very long. I made an excuse that I felt uncomfortable on the sand, and I headed off to walk along the seashore. I gathered small stones, I'd go into the water and swim out to a rock, and I'd sit for a while. When I'd swim back, he'd look a bit confused as if he hadn't noticed that I wasn't there.

I spent the first few days hoping he'd get bored and would want us to go to the hotel beach. Our days passed the same way. In the morning after we finished breakfast, we'd go to the beach. Most of the time he'd do crossword puzzles or doze off. He'd lie on his back, his straw hat over his face, and doze for hours. We spent our evenings at one of the tavernas. First we'd eat and then go walking along the harbour until we were tired.

3.

During the days after our arrival on the island, not only did our relationship not improve, but as the days went by, we even lost what little communication we had. Like me, Vlado probably thought this trip was a mistake.

After breakfast on the eleventh day, Vlado said we were going to the hotel beach that day. I wasn't at all surprised. He set off alone to get us beach chairs, while I went back to the room for the things we needed. I stood a few moments in front of the shelf of books. Among the books was Ivan's latest novel. I knew I wouldn't read it in front of Vlado. I read his new books at work. During breaks when everyone goes out, I usually lock myself in and read. I never read his books at home, even when Vlado's away on a trip. I keep his new books in the bottom drawer of my desk at work. I never write reviews of them. You can't be objective about someone who means a lot in your life. I grabbed a book from the top of the pile and put it in my bag.

Vlado was standing by the bar hugging two children while a woman took their picture. He was smiling. He only smiles when someone praises him. His hair was tousled, his white shirt was unbuttoned to his chest, and he was holding a pipe in his right hand. He always carries a pipe with him, even though he doesn't smoke. Whenever he has something important to say, or at least something he thinks is important – and that's most of the time – he puts the pipe in his mouth, squints one eye, and with the other gazes thoughtfully somewhere off in the distance. This way, even when he's talking about something insignifican it gives everyone else the impression that he's saying something deep. Then, when he wants to make a point, he opens his eye and looks at each person in turn, and after that says what he wanted to say. Everyone nods and then, pleased with himself, he calls out: 'Another glass of wine now for everyone!'

When he saw me standing off to the side, he let the children go and called me to join them. These are Nita India and Mila India, he pointed towards the twin girls. Nita India held out her hand to greet me, and then quickly pulled it back and looked at her sister. Mila India looked at me as if she didn't see me, then after several seconds, she also put her hand out. She tightly squeezed my hand and didn't let go. Even though they seemed the same, there was something different about them. I looked at her quizzically, while everyone stared at me. Her mother pulled her to herself and then Mila India let go of my hand. Vlado decided to interrupt this unpleasant situation and, waving the pipe, said 'And this… and this… and,' he said taking their mother's hand, 'This is their extremely beautiful mother, Ilinka Indira.' Ilinka Indira laughed with false modesty and looked at him seductively. 'She and her husband are from Macedonia. They've been living on the island for a few years already,' he said. I didn't say anything. I didn't want any new acquaintances. The last thing I wanted on this island were Macedonians who would recognise Vlado and chase after him the whole time. 'Look. Just look. Doesn't Ilinka Indira look like the widow in Zorba the Greek? See how much she resembles Irene Papas.' Whenever he complimented women, he always said the same thing. Ilinka Indira pressed her palms together and bowed to him.

She really did look like Irene Papas. Her dark tan was natural, but the loose salwar she was wearing, her green eyes – which I was sure were contacts – even the ankle chain on her right leg that jingled whenever she moved, had something completely fake about them.

Ilinka Indira looked at the sun and unexpectedly let out, 'Oooo…

it's already ten o'clock. It's time for me to go. But we'll meet up this evening at the Three Blue Boats as we agreed.' She turned first towards me, and with her hands pressed together, she bowed. Then she turned to Vlado, and bowing, winked at him. Nita India waved to us, but Mila India looked at us in bewilderment as if noticing us for the first time.

I was angry at Vlado all day. There were so many things I wanted to say to him, but I didn't have the courage. I wanted to tell him that the biggest mistake had been the day he invited me to move in with him after Ivan left our lives forever, and when I said yes and decided to stay there. And that day in the car, I should have told him I didn't want to travel anywhere with him.

The crowd and the music on the beach made me completely anxious. Vlado spent the entire day lying on his beach chair. From time to time, he'd sit up and look around to see whether anyone was looking at him. He did not mention Ilinka Indira or the children even once.

4.

Vlado began to work in the theatre several months after I moved in with him. I had already been working for a year at the university library. In the beginning, I supported him. It really bothered him that he had to depend on me financially. He was always very proud, so he kept telling me how natural it was for artists to have no money. Once he started working, he never mentioned it again. There was even that time a journalist asked him how long we'd been living together, and he told her that at the start of our relationship I had been unemployed and paying rent, so he suggested I move in with him. 'Nothing romantic', he added to avoid further questions. He knew I would never reveal that this wasn't true.

He was never beloved by his colleagues and directors. From the first year he began working in the theatre even till today, Vlado's rarely got roles, and when he does get them, it's usually minor ones. He'd always said they don't give him major parts out of vanity and jealousy. That's how he spent the first ten years of his career. But then one evening, something changed. A well-known journalist who had a TV show showed up at the theatre where Vlado worked and asked for his phone number. The journalist intended to invite a different actor, a well-known comedian, who, by chance, was also named Vlado. When Vlado showed up that evening at the show, it was too late to correct the mistake. The journalist saw him for the first time in his life. To avoid letting on that he was unprepared to speak with this Vlado, the journalist asked him ▪ imitate someone. Vlado sensed this was an excellent opportunity to do something for his career. He imitated a politician who was considered untouchable. The TV show had a huge number of viewers. The journalist then suggested that he imitate a politician on every show. He began to be invited to theatres in other cities. The original politician even mentioned in an interview that Vlado had imitated him so well he couldn't get angry. And then came the film in which Vlado had a brief appearance, but he used his popularity to draw attention to himself for those ten seconds. He became so popular that even when he didn't say anything funny, people laughed.

5.

Ilinka Indira was dressed in a black knee-length dress. It had a plunging neckline but didn't make her look cheap. Between her breasts hung a necklace with a piece of coral dangling from it. Her hair was down. She looked beautiful. She had come alone. Her husband had stayed with the girls. As soon as Vlado saw her, he jumped up and kissed her hand. Ilinka Indira reluctantly gave me her hand. I sensed she wasn't very happy to see me. I wasn't happy to be there that evening either. I would have much preferred to stay in our room and read Ivan's novel.

Ilinka Indira was talking about how she hadn't been able to find herself for a long time, until she went to India. And there, in an ashram, while she was waiting her turn to see Sai Baba, a man came out and told her that Baba was not receiving any more people. He placed sacred ash, vibhuti, in her hand. The man was Baže, now her husband. That same evening, she decided to add Indira to her name. 'I didn't see Baba, but he gave me two things: love and a new name.' She then fell silent. She stopped talking awhile and looked off into the distance. She and Vlado were already drunk. I stood up to go, but the two of them looked at me reproachfully. 'And what do you do?' Ilinka Indira asked. 'He's a literary critic,' Vlado answered. Vlado often answered for me when someone asked me a question. The other people then think I'm shy, so they don't ask any follow-up questions. But she didn't give up. 'So where do you publish your literary criticism?'

'I used to write for the newspaper *Nova Makedonija*, but now I write ɔr the journal that's published by the library where I work.' Vlado glanced at me and smiled, pleased. I hate it when he treats me like I'm not capable. Ilinka Indira waved my comment aside and gulped down her drink. Then she reached out clumsily for Vlado to pour her some more wine. 'I hate critics! I used to write poetry. I've published two collections. I always thought critics were people who didn't know how to write.' Vlado laughed out loud. I hated him intensely at that moment. I wanted to tell him he was a bad actor, but I didn't have the courage. I grabbed the bottle of wine in front of him and filled my own glass. The two of them looked at me in surprise. 'So, you don't write poetry anymore?' I asked. 'Oh, no; absolutely not! When I went off to India I began to draw. I mainly drew mandalas. But when the twins were born, I began to work with jewellery. I made this for myself,' she said pointing to her necklace with the dangling coral.

This time I chugged the whole glass of wine. I was working up the courage to say that I've always hated people like her. Every day I'm surrounded by people who dress like her, who think like her, who think they understand everything about the arts, when, in fact, it's just a put-on because they have no talent. They hide behind their weird clothes and their belief that love will save the world just to hide their own lack of talent, thinking that this way, they add to their importance when they have none. And while I struggled with myself to say this, Ilinka Indira looked at the two of us as if she had just sobered up and asked, 'Well, how did you two meet?' We both despised this question. Not that there was anything shameful in how we met, but there was always that thing between us that neither of us wanted to mention. Ivan.

'In the student cafeteria. I was in my third year at university, and he was in his second. When he came into the cafeteria, I was standing on a table reciting Petre Andreevski's poem "When I Loved Denicija".' Vlado then stood up. He blinked several times and then climbed up on the table and began to recite. All the guests in the restaurant looked at him. Ilinka Indira looked back and forth at him and me in delight just smiled at her, happy that Vlado had saved the situation. What he said was only partially true. But in this instance, it suited me. If I had had to answer, I would most likely have got flustered and I'd have told the truth. Vlado noticed that everyone was looking at him, so he continued reciting poems, in other languages as well. At one point he even began reciting in a non-existent language, which Ilinka Indira thought was Esperanto. He kept reciting, and I kept pouring myself more wine.

6.

I woke late. The time for breakfast had long since passed. I felt ravenous. Vlado wasn't in bed. He had neatly folded his pyjamas and placed them on his shelf. He never folds his pyjamas. He always throws them on the bed. His toothbrush wasn't in the glass in the bathroom. I sensed that something was going on. I texted him that I wasn't feeling well from all that drinking and asked whether he could bring me something to eat. I tried to reach him several times. His phone was turned off.

Sometime after lunch someone knocked on the door. I thought it was him, that he had forgotten his keys. It wasn't him at the door, but the receptionist, who handed me a bottle of wine. A slip of paper was attached to the bottle saying: *Thank you for the lovely evening! Yours, Ilinka Indira.*

I tried a few more times to get him on the phone, but still no one answered. This wasn't like him. I went back into the bathroom. I noticed that even his razor wasn't there. I looked carefully through the closet where he hung the shirts and pants that he wore in the evening when he went out. Then I looked through the drawer with his socks and underwear as well. Everything was arranged neatly, just the way I had placed them the first day. I didn't know what to do. On the balcony, from where you could see the whole beach, the two pairs of swimming shorts he wore were already hanging on the line. That meant he wasn't on the beach either. I went back to the clothes closet and looked everything over in more detail. All that was missing were the clothes he was wearing the night before, his toothbrush and his razor.

I went down to the reception and asked whether they had seen him. 'We haven't seen him since you went out last night, sir,' was the answer. When I asked how I had got back, they answered, 'A woman in a black dress. She took you up to your room.'

I returned once again to the room to see whether the car keys were there. They were lying in the drawer of his night table right beside his mobile phone. He hadn't even taken his phone.

On my way out, one of the young women at the reception told me that he might have gone into town, about two kilometres from the hotel. There's a big market there every Friday, and even though it had most likely been over for quite some time already, maybe I should go look for him there. He has never gone to a market in his life. I always do the shopping. He doesn't even go to the supermarket.

The car was hot from sitting in the sun. I had absolutely no idea why I was going there. If he had wanted to see the market, he would surely have taken the car. Maybe he's with someone else. With Ilinka Indira… with her husband…

* * *

At the market, except for the dirty stalls and the few people cleaning up the chaos to get the street back to normal, there was no one else. I didn't know where to go. I knew I wouldn't see Vlado there.

On my way back, I drove through the centre of the town and merged onto the old road which heads towards the beach. When the sea opened in front of me, I slowed down and kept my eyes on the people swimming and sunbathing. But Vlado wasn't among them. Near the end of the beach, right by the hotel, I saw the twins playing tennis on the shore. Nita India hit the ball to Mila India. The ball flew over her shoulder and landed in the sea. Several seconds later she waved her racket in the air. When she realised she was waving at emptiness, she turned to look for the ball in the water. Ilinka Indira came out of the water and gave it to her. Now it was Mila India's turn to serve the ball. First she swung several times in the air and then hit the ball. Nita India hit it back to her. The ball fell at Mila India's feet. She stood there with her racket raised and waved it in the air again several seconds later. Ilinka Indira took the racket from her and showed her several strokes. Mila India stood in position with one knee bent, then, after a few swings at the air, she hit the ball so hard that it flew towards me. Everyone looked at me. I threw the ball back to them and quickly got in the car. I did not want to run into her. I didn't want her to ask me about Vlado.

7.

I decided to stay in the hotel room and wait for Vlado. I figured he wouldn't be able to hold out and he'd come back to get a change of clothes. He couldn't stand being in the same clothes more than a day. He didn't even wear his theatre costumes twice if they hadn't been laundered. After the performance he'd bring them home and return them only after they'd been cleaned.

I spent the day on the internet, searching through registries of people who had disappeared. One of them was Ellie Papadopoulos, an editor in an Athens publishing house. She disappeared in Frankfurt five years ago. In 2013, while she was waiting for the S8 train at the Hauptwache stop, she told several publishers with whom she was attending the Frankfurt Book Fair to go on without her and that she'd go back to the hotel on the next train. She never returned. The next morning, one of the publishers who was sharing a room with her noticed that Ellie was not in her bed and decided to notify the police. On the security cameras, Ellie's colleagues could see themselves boarding the train and her leaving the station. Afterwards, all trace of her was lost.

Why Ellie had decided to leave her husband, her friends, hotel room number 327 on the third floor of the Crowne Plaza, wasn't clear to anyone until early that morning when she called a woman she met with from time to time.

The woman, Rea, stated on a program that searches for missing people, My mobile phone began to ring at four in the morning. I didn't ecognise the caller's number but I noticed right away that it was a

German one, so, another reason I thought it was her. There was silence on the other end of the line. When I asked: "who is it... who is it," the only reply I got was "It's me," and then I was cut off. The call lasted six seconds.'

'Ellie is finally happy,' her friend added. 'That day at the Hauptwache stop she left her husband, who was constantly telling her that she was fat and useless, even though she had been supporting him for years. The boring meetings with book agents, publishers, egotistical writers, all of that was left behind. She was finally free.'

I was imagining Vlado telling Ilinka Indira to take me back to the room, and him staying behind alone. Suddenly he realises something in his life isn't right, so he disappears into the darkness.

Years later, in an amusement park near the Panepistimio Station in Athens, a clown emerges from another darkness, and all the visitors gather around him. The clown is happy. Everyone loves him. He laughs. The crowd laughs too.

* * *

I decided to go out that evening anyway. The city was decorated with flags and balloons. Stalls had been set up on the sidewalk. The streets were overflowing with people. I was sure that Vlado was somewhere among them. Thousands of people I didn't know were moving towards me in an encounter like those I had been watching on the computer screen that morning in the registry of people who have disappeared. Maybe one of them is a missing person. And while someone is desperately looking for them, they're calmly eating cotton candy at the fair. In front of one of the game booths there was a man standing with his back turned shooting an apple with an air rifle. I was standing a few metres away from him. He looked a lot like Vlado. But the way he walked, the clothes he was wearing, didn't look like him at all. He turned into a side street where a small stage had been set up. The man seemed to know I was following him, so he slipped into the crowd of people recording the concert on their phones. And then I lost sight of him.

8.

When I went down to the hotel restaurant the next morning, breakfast still hadn't been set out. I sat on the terrace, with a view to the sea. I felt a ringing in my head. It was the same feeling I had had during the first days after my accident when I flipped over the railing. But then I had had Vlado with me. This morning I was alone on the terrace. There was no one else around. I felt like I was all alone in the hotel. The waiter came out of the restaurant and began setting ashtrays on the tables. I asked him to bring me a coffee, but he kept working without paying any attention to me. On the stairs leading from the beach to the restaurant I saw a black silhouette. I thought it was Vlado. And that he was coming back drunk. Anger took the place of the ringing in my head.

On the stairs an old woman appeared, holding a white cane in her right hand, while in her left she was leading a Labrador on a leash. The dog moved at her pace. There was something soothing in their gait. The old woman was dressed completely in black. Black shoes, black stockings, black dress, black purse, black glasses and a black clasp in her hair. She came up to my table and tapped several times with her cane on the chair opposite me. After assuring herself that no one was sitting there, she sat down. The dog lay down at the same time. The woman pulled a book printed in Braille from her purse. I coughed several times to signal to her that she wasn't alone at the table. The old woman didn't budge. She gently passed over the letters with her finger. I hadn't run into her in the hotel until then. I glanced at my watch. It was 6:50. There were still ten minutes until breakfast.

22

The waiter brought two coffees. He placed one in front of her, the other in front of me. He had newspapers tucked under his arm. He gave me the one in English, and her the one in Greek. I wanted to tell him she was blind, but before I could say anything, the old woman had set her book on the table and picked up the newspaper. To hide my confusion, I began to flip through my newspaper.

I folded the newspaper, the old woman got up to go. She moved with slow steps along the terrace, as if she and the dog had all the time in the world.

It was only after she left that I noticed that on the table she had left behind her Braille book. When I went to leave it with the reception, the receptionist told me that the old woman would be waiting for me that evening at the Orlando. 'She would be pleased if you brought it to her in person.'

9.

The Orlando was located at the end of the beach. When I got there, I saw there was a party going on. All the guests were disguised with masks. I was the only one without one. To enter, I had to pass through a line of people disguised as playing cards. On the platform there was a woman dressed as Alice. When she saw me, she lifted the corners of her blue dress and curtsied to me. Her wig slipped, and if it hadn't been held on by a ribbon, which was the same colour as her dress, it would have fallen off. I could tell it was Ilinka Indira by the little chain on her right ankle, which stood out against her white stocking. Out from behind her a server disguised as a fish appeared, who bowed, and behind the mask I recognised Nita India. Then a Server-Frog came out walking with unsure steps. Everyone looked at her. It was Mila India. Server-Fish tapped her with her elbow, but Server-Frog didn't bow, instead letting out a croak. Everyone laughed. But the loudest was the Hatter. Alice leaned towards me and whispered, 'Baže. My husband.' She said it so secretively as if it were forbidden to reveal people's true identities. Then everyone turned their backs to me and were joined by a group of Lobsters who were dancing in the middle of the platform.

I sat down at the bar, where a Rabbit with a broad smile was waiting for me.

'Divna… Divna Fisher,' she said and laughed so hard her ears shook as if they were real. And then, seemingly reminded of something, she pulled a watch from her vest pocket, swirled it around and glanced at it.

'I'm...' I began.

'I know who you are,' she said before I had time to finish my sentence. She took off her white gloves. She began looking for something under the bar. She removed a deck of tarot cards wrapped in a colourful scarf and placed them in front of me. 'Pick one,' she said. I tentatively stretched out my hand and pulled the first one I touched from the middle of the deck. The Rabbit looked at it a moment, then turned it towards me so I could see it too. It showed an old man in black clothing standing at a grave. 'The widower. You drew the widower. This card symbolizes sorrow and everything connected with the past. In astrological terms, it represents the planet Saturn; its zodiac sign is Sagittarius, the archer, and it has Earth elements. The grave symbolises sorrow and memory. The black clothing, loneliness and solitude. The falling leaves symbolize the passing of time. Pick another card,' she said and stretched her hand out to me. She had long nails painted in a garish violet colour. On each finger were several rings. All in different colours. 'I don't want to,' I said. But she persisted. She held the cards out. When she saw that I really wouldn't take one, she gathered the pile and wrapped them up again in the scarf. Then she put her white gloves back on. 'Where did you learn all that?' I asked before she had time to spring something else on me. 'This is my second life. I inherited with it the gift of interpreting destinies and dreams. I was born as Milan. But I've always wanted to be Divna. Divna like Divine. And so, Divna Fisher. Before the war I lived in a small town in Bosnia. There were barely ten thousand people there. Life was dull. My only excitement was the movies. I didn't miss a single film until the war. When a new film was showing, I'd watch it over and over until another one came. Sometimes I saw the same film ten or twenty times. I didn't find it boring. What was boring for me was reality. When it snowed and the long winter set in, or when it rained for days in the spring, I was the only one sitting in the cold hall. I watched films constantly until the beginning of the war.

But then the theatre was destroyed, and I was drafted into the army. Until then I had only ever seen a rifle in a film. But lucky for me, that very same night, with a friend's help I fled first to Slovenia, and then to Austria. There I became Divna. Divna Fisher. But I still felt empty. I was missing something. That feeling stayed with me until I met Sanchi.

'After I got a work permit, I began working for a hotline. One evening he called me. Sanchi, that is.' The Rabbit pointed towards a Caterpillar, who was sitting in the corner smoking a hookah. 'When he called, he told me he just wanted to have a conversation with me. We could, for example, talk about movies. And so, every evening he'd call me and we'd talk about movies. After about a year-long conversation, Sanchi invited me to the movies. Ever since then, we've watched films together every night. When the war ended, I lost my status as a temporary asylum-seeker, and I had to return to Bosnia. Sanchi couldn't accept the fact that he wouldn't see me anymore, so he suggested that we seek our fortune in some new place. He had come to Vienna on a scholarship to study medicine. After he graduated, he was supposed to return to India. While he was waiting in line at passport control in the airport, he realised he didn't want to go back, that his life was in Austria. He stayed illegally. He worked as a walking billboard for the movie theatre we went to. One of his co-workers, who was from the island, suggested we come here. We've been here for twenty years already. In the beginning, the Orlando was a summer movie theatre. But then we also began to organise parties. Here I found my happiness. How couldn't I be happy with all these wonderful people?'

The Rabbit, or Divna Fisher, stopped talking. She went to the refrigerator and took out several lemons. She began to slice them in circles. She popped a slice into her mouth and began to suck on it, and then, as if something again occurred to her, she took another slice and gave it to me. 'Tell me something about yourself,' she said. 'There's nothing to tell,' I said. 'My life isn't as interesting as yours.' 'No, no, no.

there are no uninteresting lives, only untold ones. Each person is a story. Each one. Over there, for example, is Kareta,' she said pointing to the Turtle, who was trying to keep in step with the Lobsters, but because of her short legs and the shell on her back she moved clumsily. 'Kareta grew up in Cetinje, in Montenegro. She lived there until she was twenty. She read books for days on end. She especially liked books which had to do with the sea. She always had a longing to visit the sea, even though she lived only thirty kilometres away from it. Kareta was always teased because of her dwarfish size and her hunchback. She'd spend days shut up in her room with a book in her hands. Other than reading, travel was her great passion. One day she gathered her courage to face the world and decided to go to Herceg Novi to see the mimosa trees. But when she tried to buy her ticket, the woman at the ticket office didn't even notice her because the counter was higher than she was. Then one of the passengers in the waiting room said, "The turtle is speaking," and everyone began to laugh. She never saw the mimosa trees, but she fell in love with turtles forever. Especially sea turtles. From reading about them, she learned about the species *Caretta caretta*. She saw on the internet that there was a society called Save the Turtles which Sanchi and I lead. This is her second life.'

The Rabbit suddenly fell silent and glanced somewhere over my shoulder. A man in a baby mask which resembled a pig was standing a few steps behind me. When the Pig-baby saw that we were looking at him, he went off to join the Lobsters, who were still dancing. Alice came up to me and tugged at me to go and dance. The Cards and the Lobsters were standing in a circle, chanting; Alice said, 'There's no escape, everyone is waiting for you.' I got up although I didn't know how to dance. I consoled myself that it was better being seen by these people I didn't know. When I got up on the platform, everyone began dancing. One of them yelled, 'Joy!' And as if in a chorus, everyone else began shouting 'Joy, joy.' I began swaying distractedly. I was trying to imitate the Hatter's movements. The Turtle came up beside me and lifted one of her legs so high that she flipped over. Her shell was on the ground, and like a real turtle, she began fluttering her legs in the air. The Cheshire Cat came and flipped her over so she could get up. The Turtle got back on her legs and continued dancing. When I saw that no one was looking at me, I went back to the bar.

'And your story?' asked the Rabbit as if she had just been waiting for my return. 'If I knew how to write stories, I would have been a writer and not a critic,' I answered. That pleased her, and she laughed. 'We are all spiritual beings. But the only ones who understand are those chosen by the cosmos. The others die without becoming conscious. One morning you will wake, and you will no longer feel your own body. In the mirror you will see your hands, your feet, your face as if they belonged to someone else. Then you will begin to understand that you are not just a body and that your mission in this life is different from that of others. In the beginning you won't want to accept that, you'll say to yourself, why me? In the end you will be grateful to the cosmos for choosing precisely you to live a second life. Take Andreas over th she pointed to the Pig-baby. 'When we opened the Orlando, he p all of these pictures.' And she turned to the wall behind her middle was the peace symbol of the hippie movement surrounded by inscriptions in English: *Today is life tomorrow Love, Hippie – Hippie* and lots of flowers. There was someth in the Pig-baby. I couldn't connect all these cheerful col

'Andreas was the sixth child in his family. He has His parents had decided not to stop until they gave b when he was born, they placed all their hopes in him to become like his great-grandfather, who Arkadi monastery, on the island of Crete. On monastery was attacked by the Turkish arm Marinakis, refused to leave with the other

'The Turks attacked and planted explosives around the monastery. There were also villagers inside. The victims, who died defending the monastery, became a symbol of Greek independence. His mother was particularly proud of this ancestor of hers. Her grandfather fought in the Greco-Turkish War of 1919 to 1922. And when, in '41, Greece was attacked by the Germans who had come through Yugoslavia and Bulgaria and occupied most of the country. The king and the government fled to Crete, her father fought to the end in the battle for Crete. Andreas's mother loved to tell all these details.

'His sisters weren't allowed to go to school. All the money was saved so when Andreas grew up, he would be able to go to the military academy. But when he went to Athens to enrol at the school, instead of doing what was expected, he enrolled in the arts academy. Up until the fourth year of his studies, he hid this from his parents, especially from his mother. When they found out, his parents stopped sending him money, and he had to return to Crete. His mother continuously scolded him for being useless and shaming all his ancestors. As the only male heir, his obligation was to become a general, but he had decided to paint flowers.

'On 16 November 1973, Andreas set off to Athens to join the students who had occupied the Polytechnic School and were demanding an end to the military dictatorship and a return to democracy. It was his last chance to become a son worthy of the family tree in the eyes of his mother. He planned to come out of the Polytechnic as a revolutionary, and in return he would ask his mother to let him continue his studies in the Arts Academy. But about halfway there, a terrible storm came up. The sea was so wild, it seemed as if it would swallow the boat at any moment. The rocking of the boat made Andreas seasick, as it did most of the other passengers. He vomited nearly the entire way. When the boat finally arrived in Athens, he decided to get a room in a hotel in Piraeus to rest up, and then join his colleagues.

'On 17 November 1973, at 3:30 in the morning, when the fence was destroyed by a tank and the army entered the Polytechnic faculty, Andreas, exhausted from the trip and seasickness, slept through the revolution. The next morning, when he woke, he learned from the receptionist what had happened. He returned to Crete that same day and was left to live with a sense of guilt that he had not been with his colleagues that morning, that he had failed his mother's expectations, and most of all, that he would never become a painter. Even after his mother's death, he couldn't stop blaming himself. But one morning he woke up and understood that his mission in the world was not to do what others expected of him or what he himself had expected, but what the cosmos had prepared for him.' With her index finger Divna Fisher pointed up as if pointing to the cosmos.

Loud applause could be heard behind my back. The Rabbit excitedly called out: 'Here are The King and Queen,' and she began to clap with joy.

The blind woman that I had seen in the morning on the hotel terrace was standing at the entrance, leading an old man who was also blind. Everyone gathered in a circle. The two old people began to dance. She led him as if he were a doll. His movements were slow and tentative.

The Rabbit looked at them with admiration. It seemed to me that when they appeared, everyone became even happier. Even the Pig-baby lost his gloomy expression. It was as if the heaviness inside him had lifted with their arrival.

'Who are these people?' I asked the Rabbit. 'They are Elena and Kosta. He is a retired lawyer, and she's a teacher. He's twenty years older than her. Elena was the only one in the area who knew how to type on a typewriter. They spent whole days together. That's how they fell in love. She finished teachers' college and began to work as a teacher. After work she'd go to his office and help him. Over the course of time, Elena began wearing dark glasses, because of her love for him.'

The Rabbit fell silent. From her vest pocket, she took out the watch. 'Ah, I've spoken too long. You're already late,' she said, and, from the other pocket, she took out a key and handed it to me. 'Behind the bar you'll see some stairs. On the left side is the bathroom, and on the right is the exit you need to go through.'

She gave me the key with such excitement, as if she were in some parallel universe.

10.

The door led to an open terrace. With uncertain steps I moved through the darkness. Above me shone the stars, the Moon, and the Milky Way. Below me the sea was striking the rocks.

I felt a warm breeze on my neck. Shivers ran down my spine. I began to step forward. There was no railing. Just one step more separated me from death. And then, as in a dream, I saw my whole life before me. I saw myself standing there on the edge. But I didn't see the person standing behind me.

'I was waiting for you to come,' he said.

SEARCH

1.

Vlado was sitting at the edge of the restaurant terrace at a table which was just about in the sea itself, reading *Other Voices, Other Rooms* by Truman Capote. It was the same book Ivan had been reading before he left. The same edition. On the back cover there's a photograph of Capote. Ivan always told me that I reminded him of Capote. Vlado, as if noticing the surprised look on my face, set the book down on the table. 'I left you a note at the reception, did they give it to you?' I nodded. 'He didn't notice you?' he said looking me straight in the eye, the way Ivan used to. 'Which he?' I asked, confused. 'Vlado, of course.' I shook my head.

'Why did you leave?' I asked, my voice trembling. 'Then, twenty years ago.' I couldn't finish the sentence. Vlado was caught off guard. He wasn't prepared for that question. Maybe because he didn't know the answer either. That question was a mistake. Surely, he also felt that pain. I saw him knit his brows. Vlado always has that look on his face when he's annoyed. 'Maybe I should go,' I said. He didn't say anything to me. I realised that I really did need to leave him alone.

In university, Ivan and I often went to student performances to see Vlado. We always sat in the first row. When he saw us from the stage, Vlado would gain confidence and try to distinguish himself even more. After his performances, he always told us that he was acting just for us.

When Ivan disappeared from our lives and Vlado began to work in a theatre, I went less and less often. There was a show in which he was to appear in the first act and the last. When he came out on the stage for the second time, he totally changed his lines. He was supposed to say something short, one sentence. He delivered a whole monologue. He drew all the attention to himself. At the end, when he came out for a bow, he got the longest applause. Even his colleagues applauded him bewilderedly. I was the only one looking at him disapprovingly. Several months later, when Ivan published his first novel, *Through the Dense Forest at Night*, I recognised in one of the chapters the segment that Vlado had recited at the end of his performance. I never did find out how he knew that chapter of the novel, since it hadn't yet been published, and we weren't in touch with Ivan.

After that evening, I went less and less often to the shows he performed in, and I finally stopped going at all. But Vlado never gave up. He kept leaving me tickets for every premiere.

That evening when I found him on the Orlando terrace, I became part of the drama he was directing, in which he and I were the only actors. At first, I didn't even recognise him. He had completely changed. The clothes he wore, the way he spoke, his body language, everything was different. And yet, at the same time, every word, every movement was familiar to me. The more I looked, the more I recognised Ivan in him. I didn't know whether in the twenty years I was ignoring his performances and imitation shows, something had changed, but I could see that Vlado had become a superb actor. He was doing a perfect imitation of Ivan.

I was afraid of what would happen next. I ran up the stairs, but before I left, the Lobsters dragged me onto the stage. There, the turtle was still dancing, and she kept knocking into me with her shell. I managed to get away and run to the beach. I spent the evening sitting in a beach chair. I didn't want to return to our hotel room. I was afraid of having to face him. I left only as dawn was breaking. He was sleeping in the bed. The pants and shirt he had been wearing the evening he disappeared were tossed on the chair. As I lay down beside him, he asked me, half-asleep, and without turning over, 'You here?' And then, without

waiting for an answer, he began to snore. It was the same old thing
again. The old Vlado.

* * *

When I woke up, he wasn't there. He had left a glass of orange juice
and a plate of fruit on the night table. When I picked up the glass, I
saw that he had left me a note:

'I didn't want to wake you; I've gone for a walk. See you at lunch.
Vlado.' Later, at the reception, a new note was waiting for me: 'I'm
waiting for you at the beach. Ivan.' The handwriting had changed. The
letters in the second note were elongated, just the way Ivan wrote.

Our first meeting had not gone well because of my mistake. I
shouldn't have asked that question. I had to say something that
connected us, not something that divided us.

Ivan's departure had hurt us both. I couldn't make more mistakes at
our next meeting. There weren't many days left until the end of our
vacation. I couldn't allow myself that luxury any longer.

While I was walking along the street on the way to the beach, I saw
Ilinka Indira with her children, together with the Turtle, the Rabbit,
and the old blind man and woman. There were other people with them
I didn't know. 'Let's save the planet Earth!' was written on the banners
they were carrying. Nita India and Mila India had their hair in braids
like Greta Thunberg. They were carrying banners which read: 'Join the
march against climate change.' Kareta, the Turtle, was holding a small
aquarium which had a picture of a turtle pasted on it with the words:
'Donate for the *Caretta caretta* turtles.' The group asked everyone who
passed by to put something in the aquarium. I wanted to get away from
them, but Ilinka Indira was faster than I was, and she called me to join
them. I told her that I had to go, but she called out loudly, 'Let's save
the planet Earth!' and she didn't even notice when I ran off.

2.

'What are your plans for today?' I asked when I saw that his eyes were open. He looked at me in surprise. Like he didn't know what I was talking about. 'What are you planning to do today?' I asked again. You could read the disappointment on his face. This was a second mistake. He knew my question was about when I would be free of him and when I would see Ivan.

He didn't say a word all morning. I was afraid that he wanted to punish me and that he would stop the game. 'Should we go to the beach?' I said with false gaiety. I wanted to give the impression that his presence was important to me. But without answering, he took his backpack and left.

In his every step I saw how listlessly he moved. He was surely disappointed that I had destroyed in a single sentence even that slender hope we had of improving our relationship. I was simply afraid that I wouldn't see Ivan in him anymore. It was as if the curtain had come down, and the two of us found ourselves on opposite sides of the stage. I felt like we would never appear in the same act again.

Ilinka Indira was on the beach with a man. When Vlado saw them, his mood lifted. 'This is Saffron, my spiritual brother,' she said. And she sat down on a beach chair beside us. 'Just think, the two of us were in India at the same time. In the same ashram. But we met each other here,' she added. I asked him whether he also lived on the island. I wanted to give Vlado the impression that I was interested in his friends. Saffron replied, 'Yes and no. We begin where our bodies end. This morning at dawn I was in the fields of a village in Nepal. I was leading cows to pasture. But my body was here on the island. You'll surely understand what I'm saying,' he said, turning to Vlado. 'You're an actor, you're always in the same body, but you are always someone else.' Ilinka and I glanced at him. Vlado felt important. Once again, he had his old self-assurance. 'Well, how can I put this… That's exactly why I chose the profession. There's nothing better than the challenge to be someone else.' Ilinka Indira began to applaud. 'Come on, let's all take our picture,' she said and took a phone from a folk-embroidered bag. Vlado took it and handed it to me to take their picture, while he sat in the middle of them. He threw his arms over their shoulders. Saffron and Ilinka Indira were melting in his embrace. Then he suggested they all go swimming. 'Watch our things,' he said as they set off towards the sea.

Vlado wanted to humiliate me. So I'd feel how he had felt this morning. And he succeeded. But another feeling also arose in me. When I saw how much he was enjoying himself with those two, how much attention he was giving them, I felt jealous. We never knew how to relate to each other like that. Between us there was only emptiness.

They came out of the water and sat down on the shore. Ilinka Indira spread her legs and began to gather a pile of sand in front of her. She looked like a little girl imprisoned in the body of a giant. Vlado and Saffron sat beside each other. Their shoulders were touching. From time to time one of them would say something and they'd laugh. Vlado ran his tongue along Saffron's neck. 'You're salty,' he told him. Then Saffron licked him. 'You're salty too,' he replied. Ilinka Indira had a castle between her legs. 'Let's find straws and arrange them on the top like a flag,' one of them said to her. I couldn't watch them anymore. 'You'll see about this if you return as Ivan,' I kept telling myself. 'We could put little pebbles on too,' said Saffron. He began to gather them with Vlado. When one of them would find a pebble, he'd put it in the other's hand. They were all gathered around the castle decorating it.

'Come on, who can swim to that rock first,' said Ilinka Indira. And they all threw themselves into the water. When their bodies began to disappear in the distance, I went over to the castle and kicked it apart. I didn't want any of it to remain. I only returned to my beach chair after even the smallest clump of sand had disappeared.

When they got out of the water, they didn't even notice it wasn't there. They came over to the beach chairs and began gathering up their things. Vlado also gathered up his things. 'We'll see each other this evening,' he said to me.

All three of them left together.

3.

Vlado continued to ignore me the following day. When I woke up, he was coming out of the bathroom. He had showered. He tossed the wet towel he had wrapped around him onto the bed. These habits of his always got under my skin. I wanted to shout at him to hang it on the balcony to dry, but I was afraid I would make our relations even worse. He put on his Bermudas and the short-sleeve shirt he wore in the evenings. 'Want to order breakfast for the room?' I asked him in a gentle voice, but inside me everything roiled with nervousness. He didn't answer right away. He went into the bathroom, and I heard him spraying on cologne. 'I'm having breakfast with Saffron. You can eat in the room if you want,' he said and went out. He left the door ajar. He never fully closes a door. I took the wet towel off the bed and threw it at the door. I was so angry that I wanted to throw all his things down onto his head when he passed below the balcony.

I showered and I also got dressed for going out. I put on the olive-green T-shirt I had worn to a party. That evening, Vlado had been drunk and told me that I looked so good in it that he wanted to tear it off me. There were sparks of passion in his eyes. It was only when he was drunk that he expressed his emotions. But those were the moments when he was most repulsive to me. The thought of him licking my neck, making it slimy, of him clumsily lying on top of me, his body out of control from the alcohol, made me want to vomit. That's why I hadn't worn it since.

I suspected I would find them at the Orlando. They were sitting at the bar. When I entered, Vlado's hand was on Saffron's back. Ilinka Indira was sitting across two chairs. When she saw me, she greeted me listlessly. Vlado didn't even look at me. There was a bottle of Jameson standing between them. They were already half-drunk. I sat down at the other end. I asked Divna Fisher to make me a strong cocktail. Behind the bar she mixed drinks, whatever came to hand. 'This is the PM-pollution cocktail. It works really quickly. It'll knock you out fast,' she said and handed me a glass with little umbrellas and other bright-coloured decorations dangling from it. I drank a big gulp and felt the burn in my chest. Divna Fisher went to the other end of the bar. 'I have something for you,' she said to them. She pulled the tarot cards out of the colourful scarf. 'Pick one,' she said in a tone radiating with authority. Vlado and Saffron looked at each other and started to laugh. 'Come on, take one,' now it sounded like a command. They pulled out one card together and showed it to her. 'Lovers. This card represents love, passion and dedication to another person. The card depicted the emotional connection of a man to two women.'

'What else does it mean?' asked Saffron, impatiently. 'If you get involved in a new love relationship, be aware of the lover's warning. Namely, don't fall in love with love, it can be a great delusion.'

I took some long sips one after the other. 'Hahaha,' I burst out laughing. I could no longer hide my anger. Vlado leaned over all three of them and whispered something to them. I acted as if I couldn't care less. But I was dying to know what he had told them. Suddenly, they all began acting differently together. And Vlado changed. He was no longer Vlado, but Ivan. He acted like him. He spoke like him. That bothered me even more. But when I saw him hugging Saffron and making him laugh, I no longer had control of myself. I took my cocktail glass, which had a little bit left in it, and went towards them. I felt dizzy while I walked. Everyone looked at me with surprise. I tossed the glass in his face. 'This was supposed to be our game. How can you hug this guy?' I shouted at the top of my lungs. Vlado just looked at me with pity.

That's the last thing I needed. I wanted to douse him in something else, but I had nothing handy. 'Baby, baby, take it easy, come on, let's take a walk,' said Divna Fisher, and she led me towards the street. We went out to the beach. 'Get in the water, you'll feel better,' she said. She went in with me. She held me under my arms and pulled me through the water as if she were teaching me to swim. When I was a bit better, she brought me back to the hotel.

I sat out on the terrace of the hotel restaurant all afternoon and evening. I hated myself for humiliating myself in front of all those people. I especially couldn't forgive myself for showing such weakness in front of Vlado. I felt at the same time that I had ruined everything. I was prepared that he'd come, or even worse, that he wouldn't even want to see me, and he'd just send someone else to get his things. All I needed to do at that moment was to show at least a bit of dignity, if I had any left in me.

I had already given up both Vlado and Ivan.

4.

When I went down to breakfast, Vlado was already sitting there eating. I quickly grabbed a fried egg and a piece of bread and sat down next to him. He was behaving totally normally. He was his old self again. 'I am going to the Orlando. Ilinka Indira is preparing some sort of performance, and I've got to help her. I'll be back in the afternoon,' he said and left without finishing his breakfast. I sat a while longer, then went to the reception. There were no messages for me. I told the receptionist that I would be on the terrace, and if anyone left something for me, to please bring it right away.

I kept glancing towards the door. I was expecting the receptionist to appear at any moment. Coming down the stairs that led to the beach was the blind old woman. This time she was dressed entirely in green. Even the dog's leash was green. Her glasses were also green. She approached my table, tapped her cane several times on the empty chair, then pulled it out and sat down. At the same moment, her dog lay down under the table. The old woman took out the same Braille book and began to read. I took a newspaper from the next table but didn't open it. I couldn't take my eyes off her.

When she finished her coffee, she got up and pulled an envelope from her bag. She left it on the spot where she had been sitting. When I saw that she was heading to the beach, I opened it. *I will be waiting for you at 12:30 in the Three Blue Boats right beside the Orlando. Ivan.*

* * *

Vlado and I settled ourselves at a table from where I could see the Orlando. Ilinka Indira was explaining something to a group of people seated in a circle. The only one I recognised was Divna Fisher. Sitting beside her was a man in a diving suit, holding a giant sea sponge in his hand. 'They're preparing a performance. It's a play about the consequences of global warming,' said the waiter as he handed us a menu.

'This is the only vegan restaurant on the island, that's why I wanted us to eat here. Veganism is my battle against global warming,' said Vlado. I couldn't believe I was hearing this from him. Whenever he was out somewhere and there was at least one vegetarian, he'd begin to tell jokes about them. A few years ago, his colleague invited us to his villa. We were supposed to spend the whole weekend together. When we got there, he and his wife were already there. The grill was lit and there were peppers and squash roasting on it. 'These are for Melita, but I have something more substantial for us,' Ivo told us and winked. Vlado happily sat down at the table in the yard and began drinking. By the time the food was ready, Vlado was already drunk. As he watched the wife serving herself some vegetables, he crossed himself and said, 'May the *Anima mundi* forgive me,' and he jabbed his fork into the largest pork chop. Everyone laughed. I laughed too. Though I didn't think it was funny. When he saw that his joke was a hit, Vlado began to repeat it every time he took some meat. When it became tedious, Melita told him that it was no longer interesting and that he had to change the subject. But he didn't stop. He continued to tell jokes and laugh at them himself. 'When Ivo cuts the grass, does your mouth water?' he asked with a laugh. Melita began gathering the empty dishes. I offered to help her. 'I can do it myself,' she said and disappeared into the kitchen with the plates. Vlado didn't stop. Ivo got up and said, 'I'll go calm her down,' and he winked at us. But he returned alone. I said I was tired and was also going to bed.

Ivo and Melita argued all night. She blamed him for not defending her while his friend was attacking her. If my friend had behaved like that towards you, I would have reacted immediately,' she shouted at him. At one point she left the villa crying. He begged her to come back. He assured her that Vlado would apologise. The argument moved out into the yard until I heard a car leaving.

The next morning Vlado didn't remember anything. Ivo told us that there was a problem with the children, so Melita had had to return to Skopje immediately. We left that day as well.

As I watched him eating that veggie burger made of broccoli and lentils, I wanted to tell him the same joke he had told Melita. But I was afraid it would ruin the game like the day before. Now he wasn't Vlado, but Ivan.

'Eat,' he said when he saw me looking at him.

'Since when have you been a vegan?'

'For twelve years already,' he said.

I couldn't remember whether Ivan really was a vegan. And whether I had even known that term back then. I came from a small town. I lived in the student dorm. I only ate in the student cafeteria. Sometimes I sold some of my vouchers and used the money to buy books. My mother and grandmother sent me money, but it wasn't enough for me to do anything. I avoided socializing with my colleagues. I never went to a café with them, and I never went out in the evenings. I spent most of my time in reading rooms. Until I met Ivan during the class on the American short story. He was always different from the others. I wanted to be like him. I wanted to have his self-assurance, to dress like him, to think like him, to speak like him, to have read the books he had read.

We had to write an essay about a short story from American literature that had left the greatest impression on us. I wrote about 'Cat in the Rain', by Hemingway. After the course, Ivan told me it was his favourite story too, and that he had wanted to write about it, but had decided at the last minute on 'Miriam', by Capote. He wanted to know everything about me. Where I came from, why I had decided on studying comparative literature, everything I had read.

'It looks like you're not hungry,' he said to me.

'You can eat my burger too if you'd like,' I told him. He pulled the plate towards himself and began to gobble it up greedily.

Towards the end of the first year, Ivan's parents invited me to lunch to get acquainted with me. They lived in a large apartment in the centre of the city. There were books everywhere. On the shelves, on the tables, on the chairs, on the floor. There were souvenirs from their travels, pebbles from summer vacations, artworks, designer lamps and vases. They went to concerts, exhibitions, to the theatre. They were both university professors. They spoke about human rights, about the rights of animals, they had gay friends, they listened to jazz.

We lived in two rooms. There were just the three of us. My grandmother, my mother, and I. When my mother was in her third year of high school, my grandmother and grandfather sent her on a youth work action. She came back with me in her belly. When my grandparents found out, it was already too late for an abortion. After I was born, my grandfather died. From shame, my grandmother used to say.

We didn't buy books. That was a luxury we couldn't afford. When my mother would get paid for several months' work in the textile factory where she worked, she'd buy a romance novel from the traffic kiosk. That was the only thing my grandmother would let her buy for herself because there was a crossword puzzle at the back which she'd solve. My mother often had insomnia. She'd lock herself in the bathroom and read until the alarm clock rang for her to get up and go to work.

She never bought anything for herself. She gave all the money to my grandmother. On International Women's Day, 8 March, she'd give my mother some money to get new stockings and go to the hairdresser. Once I asked for some money so I could get her a present. She told me that I should buy her stockings, too, since it was the least expensive thing. Then, for the rest of the year she kept telling her, 'Lucky you! Two pairs of stockings, while I only have one pair, and they're patched.' She always made lunch to last two days so she wouldn't have to spend money on electricity the next day. It was always the same meals. Even the smallest change upset her.

The only trip my grandmother ever took was one International Women's Day, when my mother was seven years old. To Venice. All that she had left from that trip was a small gondola which stood on the shelves behind a glass door, and a single photograph. She's standing in St Mark's Square, in the middle of a flock of pigeons, her right hand is raised, most likely holding food for the birds. She's smiling. It's only in that photograph that I've seen her laughing. The whole time we lived together, she was always gloomy. If she saw my mother smiling, she'd look at her with reproach. Then my mother would have a guilty conscience. Laughing was for rich people. We had no right to laugh.

After that lunch at Ivan's, I decided not to go home for the summer holiday. I couldn't endure their unhappiness. I wanted to forget about home, the city, the way we spoke.

Vlado and I never spoke about our pasts. I knew nothing about his childhood, and he knew nothing about mine. In the beginning, while his parents were still alive, they'd come visit us. While they were there, I would try to be seen as little as possible. I never got to know them very well. My mother and grandmother never came to see me. The first time Vlado's parents came to our place, I went home. I couldn't bear being under the same roof for two days with people I didn't know.

My trip to my childhood home was clearly a mistake. I despised the city and the people. Nothing had changed. Time had stood still. Everything was the same as when I left. Faces worn out from the battle with life. Women whose lives had been spent waiting. When my mother opened the door, I didn't recognise her. Half her teeth were missing. Her hair had turned white. She cried when she saw me. Then she hugged me a long time. She smelled of rakija. I didn't know my mother had started drinking. My grandmother was lying on her bed. Her hands were tied to the bed frame with bandages. 'She has dementia. I have to tie her down. She almost lit the apartment on fire,' my mother said. I only nodded. I knew they lived humbly. Other than my grandmother's pension, they had no other income. While I was living with them, my mother worked in several textile factories, but she never found other work.

The apartment smelled of mould and stale air. Maybe it had smelled like that before, but now the smell split my nostrils. My mother opened the refrigerator. Inside, there was just some margarine and a bottle of rakija. She immediately shut it in embarrassment. 'Why didn't you tell me you were coming? I would have made something.' I just shrugged my shoulders. I didn't know what to say. I pulled out some money to give to her. But she pushed my hand away ashamed.

'Cunt! Cunt!' my grandmother shrieked, giggling. We all fell silent and looked at the branches of the linden tree striking the windows of our apartment on the third floor, in a forgotten city.

'Fluffy, do you remember Fluffy?' my mother called out with delight, happy that she finally remembered something that connected us. Fluffy was a little dog we found in a garbage container, tied in a bag, just as I was beginning high school. Shame poured over me. After I left, not only had I never thought of the two of them; I had never even thought of Fluffy. 'Fluffy's dead,' my mother said. 'Do you remember Atse? The policeman on the first floor?' I nodded, even though I couldn't recall him. 'Well, he threatened your grandmother and me. He said if we didn't get rid of Fluffy, we'd have him to tangle with. Fluffy had crapped in front of his door.' 'Crap! Crap! The cunt craps,' my grandmother shouted and laughed even louder. 'He's a police officer. You don't mess around with a policeman,' my mother sadly said to me. We fell silent again. I wanted to ask what happened next, but I didn't have the courage.

A moment later, she started up again. 'Do you remember Ile? The hunter in the entryway next to ours? Well, I gave Fluffy to him, and told him to take him into the forest when he went hunting and leave him there. Ile took him, but it seems he was afraid that the dog might come back so he just took aim…' and my mother fell silent. I could see she was struggling to hold back her tears. 'Fluffy just stopped right in front of the rifle.'

I didn't want to hear any more. I told her that I had to catch the bus back. I felt pity and contempt at the same time. I shouldn't have come back. I didn't belong there anymore. As I was hurrying to return to my life with Vlado, my mother sensed we would never see each other again and hugged me tightly. From her mouth came the stench of rotten teeth and rakija. 'I have to go,' I said. She said nothing. 'Cunt! Cunt!' shouted my grandmother. I set off quickly to get away.

After that summer when I visited my grandmother and my mother, something inside me broke in two. I first had that feeling when Ivan left, but then it only grew stronger.

I never went to see them again. I knew nothing about them. For a long time after that visit, I tried to forget the smell, my grandmother's voice, Ile the hunter's rifle. It was many years later when I read in a newspaper:

In the city B., on Dame Gruev Street, tenants reported that a terrible smell was emanating from an apartment on the third floor. Apparently, when the police entered, they found a dead old woman, and her daughter, who was sitting beside her. The first aid team determined that the old woman had been dead for two months. The body was taken to the morgue, and the woman was given professional help. Police Officer A., who lives in the same building, revealed that this was all about a dysfunctional family.

I crumpled the paper and threw it away so Vlado wouldn't see it. I didn't want him to see that 'dysfunctional family'. That wounded me more than the death of my grandmother. Even if my mother had wanted to contact me, she didn't have my number. I didn't even know if they had the same telephone number or whether it had been cut off long ago, since they had no way to pay the bills.

It was New Year's when the phone rang. Vlado and I were getting ready for a party. It was Ile. Ile the hunter. 'Your mother died,' he said. 'How did you get my number?' was the only thing I managed to say. 'The burial is tomorrow at 12:00,' he said, and hung up. The next day I sat at the bus station watching the buses come and go. I didn't have the courage to return to that city. That afternoon when I got home, Vlado was waiting to have lunch with me. We ate in silence. He didn't ask me anything. We never again mentioned that city, or my mother, or my grandmother.

* * *

Two empty plates stood defiantly between us. It was as if Vlado was trying to buy himself some time with the food. Surely, he was asking himself what Ivan would say at such a moment. 'There's a hostel nearby; if you want, we can go there,' he said after a long silence. His voice was full of longing. When I accepted the game, I hadn't even thought about physical contact. His invitation caught me unaware. 'I don't want to risk Vlado seeing me,' I said. Right then I felt that was the best answer. There was a look of satisfaction on his face. Although this was only a game, he was pleased by my answer, which showed him respect. If I had gone to the hostel, it would have meant going with Ivan, not Vlado. 'Ok,' he said, 'tomorrow at ten o'clock, I'll be waiting for you on the wild beach.'

5.

To get to the wild beach, I had to make my way through a forest of pine trees. I was very nervous. I had never been unfaithful to Vlado before. I didn't consider the Deni 25 incident as being unfaithful. After one of our quarrels, I installed Tinder. I hadn't actually planned to meet anyone. The app was more to demonstrate to myself that I was desirable. That quickly changed when I got a text. 'I know who you are,' said the text from Deni 25. 'I know you work in the university library. Want to meet up?' We met in a small café in the Mavrovka mall. I wanted to explain to him that I'd filled out the application out of curiosity, not for hookups.

Deni 25 and I had met before. He was working as a prompter in the theatre where Vlado was also working. At one of Ivo and Melita's parties Vlado had brought him to our table to introduce us. We were from the same city. He spoke in the same dialect I had before I decided to break off all relations with my former life. Unlike me, he was proud of his native city. He had held on to all his old habits. He spoke loudly, and constantly gestured with his hands, the way people did there.

That evening, he insisted I tell him what part of the city I used to live in. I told him that the name of the street had been changed a long time ago and I didn't know the new one. But he was persistent. I didn't want to attract everyone else's attention, so I told him the street. 'Hey, isn't that the street where the crazy lady kept her dead mother?' 'They lived in the entryway next to mine,' I said. I got up saying I was going to the bar for a drink. But he didn't give up.

'That stench must have reached the apartments in your entryway too.'

'I don't know,' I answered. 'I was lucky I wasn't there,' I said, and left.

'Vlado told us that you're really great at sex,' he told me that day in the café, smirking. I didn't believe him. Vlado and I went everywhere together, and everyone knew we were a couple, and, except for a few journalists who would ask him questions about us, everyone else respected our privacy. Vlado hadn't even told his parents. In the beginning, they often came to our place, but they thought we were roommates. Then, as they got older and couldn't travel, he visited them.

'What do you want from me?' I asked him. He pulled his chair close to mine and began touching me. First my knee, then my cock. He undid my zipper and stuck his hand in my pants.

'Let's go down to the garage and I'll give you a quick blowjob.'

'I don't want to,' I said. But he wouldn't give up. I pushed his hand away. When I got up to go, he said, 'I know that crazy woman was your mother.'

* * *

It didn't take me long to find Vlado. He was sitting on a rock. Beside him was spread a white towel embroidered with the insignia 'Hotel El Greco'. I stripped naked and sat on the towel. The feeling that I was being unfaithful to Vlado bolstered my shaky self-confidence. 'Aren't you going to get undressed?' I asked him. A look of surprise crossed his face. He took off his clothes and sat down next to me. Our bodies were touching. I felt excitement and my heart beating. I put my hand on his knee and slowly began moving it up. I took the head of his cock and started rubbing it. His body began to tense up. He lay on his back and closed his eyes. I moved my hand across his balls. I slowly reached down. I stuck my index finger in his hole, then my middle finger. He let out a

53

cry of pleasure. With the tip of my tongue, I began circling the head. When it was fully in my mouth, he raised his bum and moved slowly in and out. Then he just tensed his legs and let out a soft moan. I lay beside him. 'Don't you want to come too?' he asked. He put his hand on my cock, which was still erect, and started jacking me off. But nothing was coming. 'It's ok,' I told him, and I went to rinse off in the sea. There was sand stuck to his body. It didn't bother him. He stayed there lying motionless.

I swam for a long time. He didn't move. I swam up to the rock where, just a week before, I had sought refuge. I stretched out on it. I needed to be alone.

* * *

I swam back to where he was. Vlado was still lying in the same position. I pulled his arm over to me and I lay on his shoulder. His body was hot from the sun and steaming from my moisture.

When I woke up, Vlado was gone. Two men sitting on a rock opposite me looked at me suspiciously. I went back to the hotel to shower. Vlado wasn't there. They told me at the reception that he hadn't returned.

* * *

I figured that I'd find him at the Orlando. Divna Fisher was sitting at the bar. She was alone. When she saw me, she smiled. Around her eyes was a web of wrinkles. Her skin looked dehydrated. 'I used to use organic cosmetics. Now, I don't use any cream or make-up. Just rain, wind and sun,' she said when she saw me looking at her. 'I'm looking for Vlado, I thought he was here,' I said.

'I haven't seen him since the day he was here with Saffron,' she told me. When I turned to go, she looked at me as if something had just occurred to her. 'We're having the première of our performance tomorrow. Buy a ticket while we still have some. The money we raise will go towards saving the sea turtles.' Her lips spread into a smile, and her face looked like cracked dry earth. 'Some other time,' I told her. I set off towards the Three Blue Boats. When I came in, the waiter was clearing a table. I asked him about Vlado, but he didn't remember him.

* * *

I moved between the beach umbrellas, hoping that Vlado would be under one of them. Under the umbrella which looked like it might be his, there was an old woman, whose hands were covered with age spots, rubbing her husband's back with suntan lotion. In a few minutes Vlado's hands would be on my body. The thought took my breath away. Just a few days ago the thought of lying beside him was unthinkable. His dangling penis rubbing against my skin. But now I was racing to be with him.

It was too hot for the beginning of summer. Sweat was pouring down my face. Just one more restaurant before the street came to an end. It was my last hope.

Vlado was sitting in the hotel restaurant eating steak. When I sat down at the table, he glanced at me with disinterest. 'I've never understood vegetarians and vegans,' he said, laughing with his mouth full. Once again, he was his old self. There were no coincidences with him. He had planned every step perfectly. Everything he did gave me the feeling that something was changing. Vlado had understood that without Ivan, the two of us didn't exist. He was what joined us together. That evening a fear took hold of me that one day he'd grow tired of playing both roles and I'd be left alone.

After dinner, Vlado and I went up to our room. As we climbed the stairs, I felt the same nervousness I had felt that morning. Once again, we would have to face one another. This time, with Vlado. To buy myself some time, I went into the bathroom to shower. Every time I was about to leave the room, I found something else to keep me there a bit longer. I went back to brush my teeth. Then I remembered I should wash the shorts I had worn on the beach. Then, I saw some pee on the toilet seat and began to wipe it up. When I came out, Vlado was sleeping.

6.

The summer before I met Vlado, I had moved in temporarily with Ivan. His mother and father spent the summer in their house in a village by a lake. They were supposed to return at the end of August and then the three of them would go to the sea. That was the most wonderful period of my life. We went out every night and came back drunk at dawn. We slept in his bed, which was a bit small for the two of us, so we were squeezed together, one against the other. He always placed his arm under my head, and I slept on his shoulder. Whenever I felt his breath on my neck, I felt like I was drowning. Sometimes, in his sleep, he would put his hand under my T-shirt and play with my navel. At those moments I'd always get an erection. I'd go off to the bathroom in embarrassment and wait for it to subside, then return to bed.

The last morning before his parents returned, I couldn't hold out any longer. We had gone out to Boni. There, Dee-Dee Decadence and Kitty Confidential were waiting for us. I had never seen them before. Ivan had often spoken about them. 'You'll see how wacky they are, I'm sure you'll like them.' They were sitting at the bar. When they saw us, one of them got up and dragged Ivan off to dance. 'I'm Kitty Confidential,' said the other, and from her lace purse she took some lip gloss and began applying it. 'I stole it from my sister… the bag, too… what does she need them for…' Dee-Dee Decadence lifted Ivan's shirt and began licking his nipples. He laughed with pleasure. She put her hands down his jeans. I didn't want to see this. I told Kitty Confidential that I wasn't feeling well and that I had to go outside. I sat in front of the door, hoping Ivan would get worried and come find me. When I saw he wasn't coming, I went back inside. He was still dancing with Dee-Dee Decadence. Kitty Confidential was calling out from the bar. 'Ooooo – Bite him! Bite him!' Dee-Dee Decadence knelt and bit his dick. 'Hahahaha… oooo,' shouted Kitty Confidential. When Ivan came back to the bar, he looked at me in surprise, as if he hadn't remembered we were there together. Then he pulled me by the hand and began dancing with me. I tried to imitate Dee-Dee Decadence's moves, but I felt ridiculous. I've never had a sense of rhythm. Dee-Dee and Kitty joined us and began moving me. One of them took hold of my head and began pushing it down. 'Bite it… bite it,' they called out. I knelt in front of Ivan, but I didn't have the nerve. I pulled myself out from under the hand that was pressing on me and I went back to the bar. They kept dancing, but I sat off to the side and watched. Sometime before the end, when they were tired out, they sat beside me. One of them suggested that we continue in their dorm room. Ivan agreed right away, and I had no choice but to join them. I didn't want to leave him a second with those two.

Dee-Dee Decadence and Kitty Confidential went to the bathroom to change. They were afraid to go out on the street dressed like drag queens. When they came out without their wigs and make-up, I recognised them. We lived in the same dormitory, but in a different block. They were both studying in the Art Academy. I sometimes ran into them in the student cafeteria. They were always laughing loudly.

Ivan was happy to be in the dormitory. He always said that if you haven't lived in the dorm, it's like you haven't been a student. It reminded me of the apartment building I lived in with my grandmother and my mother. I never had any privacy. I had to share my room with two roommates. There was never hot water in the showers. In winter, wind blew in from the doors and windows. When we left Dee-Dee Decadence and Kitty Confidential's room, Ivan insisted on seeing my room. It smelled of mould and stagnant air. Dust was drifting everywhere, even more visible in the morning sunlight. 'Where do you sleep?' he asked. I pointed to the only bed that had been made. The springs had come through the mattress, and they poked my back, so under the bedcover I had placed the brown blanket with two tigers on it that my mother had sent me. We lay down on it. Ivan stretched his arm beneath my head. 'I want to look at you,' he said to me. We lay with our heads turned toward each other. Whenever he looked me in the eyes, I lowered my gaze to his lips. At that moment, I couldn't hold out any longer and I kissed him. He didn't even move. He looked at me a while longer, and then he closed his eyes.

That afternoon when I woke, Ivan wasn't beside me. On his side of the pillow, he had left a small notepad with a note: 'I didn't want to wake you. I had to go. My parents are most likely back. We'll see each other in seven days. I love you, Ivan.'

7.

That summer, the days passed very slowly for me after Ivan left for vacation with his parents. At first, I didn't leave my room at all. I lay there all the time. I didn't want to leave my bed. At night I couldn't sleep, I missed his presence. On the pillow, on the sheets, I sensed his smell everywhere. One morning, I doubled over in pain with cramps in my stomach, because I hadn't eaten since Ivan left. Until that instant I hadn't felt hungry. Someone knocked on the door. 'Hi, I'm Eli. It looks like you and I are the only ones in the block. This came for you this morning, so I went from room to room looking for you.' She handed me a postcard. I thought it was from Ivan and grabbed it. But as soon as I began reading, I realised it was for someone else. Someone with the same name as me but a different last name. The postcard was from Ana on the island of Zlarin. I told Eli that it wasn't for me, and I closed the door on her.

Eli kept coming the following days. She always found an excuse to drop by. One day she suggested we go sit for a while on the benches in front of the dorm. I said yes because I thought it might help me pass the time more quickly. Eli was the second person I became friends with. We studied in the same department. And more importantly, she was a good listener. I spoke to her for hours about Ivan. And she sat and listened.

Two days before Ivan's return, I lied to Eli and told her I was going with my grandmother and mother to a spa for a few days. If Ivan came looking for me, she should tell him that I'd be back soon. I didn't want him knowing that I had stayed closeted inside, waiting for him. About halfway home, I realised that this was a bad idea. I always felt worse after visits with my family. I didn't want Ivan to see me like that. I got off the bus at the first town it stopped at. I didn't want to return to Skopje. If I went to the dorm, I'd have to explain to Eli why I was back. And Ivan could also find me, and that would ruin my plan. At the ticket counter, they told me that the closest spa was twenty kilometres away. During those few months I spent at Ivan's I had saved a little money. I figured with that money I'd have enough to pay for lodging and one meal a day.

There were no rooms at the spa. The next day there would be a single room available. I didn't know where to go. I went back to the town and looked for a hotel. One night at the hotel cost the same as three at the spa. I tried to get a student discount, but it was still too much for me. I spent the night on a bench at the bus stop. That was the first time I had ever spent a night outdoors. I was afraid that if I fell asleep someone might rob me and I'd be left without even the little I had.

In the morning, before I went back to the spa, I bought a postcard at the kiosk by the bus stop. *Dear Eli, I miss my conversations with you. My grandmother and my mother are taking the waters, while I'm enjoying the sun.* I mailed it to her. I didn't want to leave even the smallest doubt. When Ivan came, she would surely show it to him. Fortunately, the room at the spa had a terrace. I brought my mattress out and lay in my underwear in the sun. I wanted to go back with a tan. To make it really look like I had enjoyed myself. As soon as I lay down, I fell asleep. I was exhausted. When I woke up a few hours later, I was so sick I couldn't even stand. I had sunstroke. I didn't go out at all the next two days.

When I got back to the dorm, I was absolutely beat. Eli was waiting for me in front of the entrance. 'Aaah... someone was enjoying himself all night!' she called out when she saw me. I smiled, pleased. I wanted Ivan to see me like this too. I'd tell him I had been out drinking all night.

I waited for her to tell me that he had come every day to see whether I had returned. But Eli didn't stop telling me how happy she was that I had thought of her and had sent her a postcard. I couldn't wait any longer and asked whether Ivan had been looking for me. 'No one came.' A sharp pain jabbed my stomach. The ounce of strength I had seemed to disappear. 'But maybe he came when I wasn't here,' she said and began talking about something else, but I couldn't listen to her. Her words, 'No one came' echoed in my ears.

Then I looked for him for days. I went by his house. But no one was there. 'Well, doesn't he have other friends?' Eli asked me one afternoon, while she was sitting with me on the street in front of his building. And then I remembered Dee-Dee Decadence and Kitty Confidential. A student coming out of the room next to theirs told me they had moved to another block, but she didn't know where exactly. Every Saturday Eli and I went to Boni. But I didn't meet anyone there I knew.

One evening, on our return to the dorm, I saw Dee-Dee Decadence and Kitty Confidential out in the courtyard. While I watched them stumbling along drunkenly, I felt renewed hope. When they saw me, they began laughing out loud. I couldn't hold out, and I asked them right off whether they knew where Ivan was. 'Ivan?' asked Dee-Dee Decadence, and she looked at Kitty Confidential. 'I haven't seen him since that night at Boni.'

8.

It was the end of September when someone knocked on my door. The new roommates with whom I would be sharing the room still hadn't moved in. I thought it was one of them. When I opened the door, I saw Ivan. He was wet. 'Aren't you going to let me in?' he asked. 'I didn't know it was raining,' I said. 'Just like in "Cat in the Rain",' he said grinning. He pulled a postcard from the back pocket of his pants. 'I didn't know the address of the dorm, so I didn't send it to you.' He had written on it: *The day I met you everything shifted from its axis and the world resembled a picture book turned upside down.* And suddenly, the thin frost beneath my feet that I had been standing on this whole time slowly began to thaw. The entire sea with all its fish and shells appeared. Life flowed through me once again. I was no longer angry at him for anything. I began seeking different justifications for him. He had surely been thinking of me. He had wanted to return from vacation after a week, but his parents insisted on his staying longer. He had no way of contacting me. There was no telephone in the dorm. He didn't know the address where to write to me.

Ivan asked if I could lend him some dry clothes. He wanted us to go to the cafeteria so he could introduce me to someone. Along the way he kept talking about this guy. It had been a long time since I had heard him talk of someone with such excitement. 'I've fallen in love with him, you will too, you'll see!' he kept repeating. Ivan frequently changed friends. He would meet someone and then would talk excitedly about them for days, but then he'd meet someone else, and he'd forget about the previous one. I imagined it would be the same with this guy he wanted me to meet.

When we entered the cafeteria, Vlado was standing atop a table reciting Sergei Esenin's poem 'The Bitch'. His shirt was unbuttoned to his chest. He had one hand on his chest, the other in the air. His gaze was uplifted. As if he were addressing some god. Everyone was looking at him, open-mouthed. Some people had even come out of the kitchen to listen to him. One woman standing at the food counter was wiping away tears. I looked at him in amazement too.

Vlado was very charismatic. Many men and women wanted to be with him. He always said what the other person wanted to hear. He seemed to know how to get under your skin. That's how he came to be part of my life and of Ivan's. His presence never bothered me. But it was Ivan that always connected us. That became clear to both of us when several months after our meeting in the cafeteria, Ivan disappeared. My roommates had gone home for the weekend, and the three of us slept in my room. In the morning when we woke, Ivan wasn't there. I knew he had disappeared again, but Vlado had to confront his disappearance for the first time. He couldn't grasp how it was possible for someone to be with you all the time and then suddenly be gone. I knew he would return, so I wasn't too disappointed. But Vlado couldn't accept it. It was then I realised that Vlado was in love with Ivan, just as I was. Later, over time, this happened repeatedly, and Vlado also came to accept it as normal. When Ivan would return, we would continue as if nothing had happened. We never asked him where he had been or what he had been doing. Sometimes I thought when he wasn't there, he had gone to see someone else, or maybe some others, but that he would eventually disappear from their lives and return to us. In the meantime, Vlado and I would spend our free time together, we ate together, slept at each other's place, went to shows, book launches. When Ivan would disappear, we would never mention him. His absence from our lives was the same as his presence. We continued with our lives, and when he returned, we continued where we had left off. My relationship with Vlado grew tighter. If Ivan hadn't been the way he was, the two of us would probably not be together. All those years, we never spoke about our feelings. Sometimes I thought it was easier for Vlado because he had always been selfish. He always put himself before others. That's why he never deceived me during the twenty years that he and I were together. He loved himself too much. Even this game was his wish. He never asked whether I wanted it too. All those years I always just did what he wanted. I became friends with his friends, I went to parties, on trips where he wanted to go. Even during those few years when Ivan was with us, I always did what the two of them wanted to. If I had disappeared, I am not sure whether anyone would have noticed. I was like my mother and my grandmother. That day I visited them, it was like seeing myself in the mirror. I didn't have the courage to face my life. Whenever I had to make a change, I pulled back. If I had closed the door on Ivan that day in the dorm when he appeared without any explanation, if I had left Vlado and gone away, my life would have made more sense. But I was afraid to make myself disappear from Ivan and Vlado's life even as a joke, because I thought they wouldn't even notice I wasn't there. All those years I was a shadow which tagged along wherever they went.

9.

Our vacation was at its end. I had never imagined it would end so quickly. I told Vlado I was going out for another coffee, and I went to the reception to ask whether there were any messages for me. 'There isn't anything,' the receptionist said. When I returned, Vlado went to get some fruit to take to the beach before breakfast had been cleared away. I waited a bit, then set off to find him. He wasn't in the restaurant. I thought perhaps he had used that time to leave me a note. When the receptionist saw me, he told me that there was nothing for me, without waiting for me to ask.

I went to the small hotel beach. Ilinka Indira and her daughters were playing volleyball in the water. Vlado had joined them. Inside the backpack, along with the towels we placed on the beach chairs, was Ivan's latest book. I hadn't noticed Vlado putting it in the backpack. Ever since Vlado disappeared the first time, the book had also been gone. It was a short novel, and I had read it that afternoon.

Three childhood friends meet again after many years and each tells stories about their experiences together from his own perspective. Several times I recognised myself in one of the characters, who had to be me. Ivan was the one who thought he knew us so well that he could imagine what we were thinking even twenty years later. The book wasn't written to justify himself to me and Vlado. There was not a single moment of regret. Everything he wrote was to convince himself that everything that had happened between us had happened because it had to happen that way.

All four of them came out of the water. Nita India's and Mila India's lips were turning purple. As she was leaving, Ilinka Indira told us that she would leave us tickets for the performance at the reception. 'That is my small gift to you,' she said.

10.

Vlado, Ivan and I didn't discuss our feelings. There was an ocean of silence between us. I never dared ask him whether he and Ivan ever saw each other alone. Without me. After Vlado entered our lives, Ivan and I were never alone. Whenever Vlado went to his parents' house on the weekend, Ivan would go off somewhere. Once I suspected they might have gone off together, and to make sure, I went to Ivan's house. His mother opened the door. She said that Ivan would be returning any minute, so I should come in and wait. I thought he would be happy when he came home and saw me, but when he returned, I sensed he was not pleased to see me. I told him I had been bored and thought we might take a walk in the park while it was sunny. He told me that he had to study. When I got up to go, his mother insisted I stay for lunch. So I stayed. Ivan began getting nervous. While we were eating, he didn't say a single word to me. It was as if I weren't at the table. He spoke only to his mother. When he finished eating, he said he had to get back to his studying. That was supposed to be a signal for me to leave. But his mother insisted we have a coffee after lunch. When he saw me returning to the table, Ivan nervously left the room. His mother and I were there alone. I saw that she was also bewildered by his reaction. She spoke to me about him the whole time, saying that he was very diligent and that he wanted to pass all his exams on schedule. Finally, I said that I also had an exam and that I needed to get back to the library reading room to study. 'But why don't you study together with Ivan,' his mother said. 'Come with me,' she said and took me to his room. Ivan was lying on his bed, nervously tossing a ball at the ceiling. When he saw me, he threw the ball so hard that when it rebounded it hit his mother. I said I couldn't study with friends around, that I really had to go. While I was walking along the hallway, I expected him to run after me and tell me to come back. He didn't. Neither did his mother.

When Vlado got back from visiting his parents, he suggested we go to lunch together. Ivan showed up in the cafeteria. He told us he was hungry and asked whether he could get some vouchers from us so he could get some food. He was acting like nothing had happened. Later, whenever Vlado went anywhere, I didn't go looking for him. I waited for the two of them to come back. We never spoke about that visit, not even when Vlado went to Moscow for a month. Ivan and I hadn't seen each other for two weeks. One afternoon, Ivan turned up at my room. 'I was having coffee with Dee-Dee Decadence and Kitty Confidential in their room, and I dropped by to see you,' he said. I wanted to tell him that I had already agreed to get together with Eli, but whenever he glanced at me, it felt like I was suffocating. All I had to do was to hear his voice, and a rush of upheaval would spread through me like a summer forest fire. I had never learned to resist him. We spent the whole day riding the bus from one end of the city to another. Everything was back to as it had been when it was just the two of us. That evening we slept together. That was the first time since Vlado had come into our lives that we slept alone together. When I woke, Ivan was already getting dressed to go. 'It's my father's birthday. I have to be there in time for lunch. We'll see each other this evening, I'll bring you some cake,' he said as he left. But he returned only after Vlado was back from Moscow.

11.

For the next few days, I avoided the reception desk and used the back service entrance to the hotel. I knew I wasn't going to get another message. Ivan had disappeared, just as he had twenty years before. Once again it was just Vlado and me.

It had been the beginning of summer then, too. Vlado had already moved out of the dorm, and I needed to be out by September. After graduation, we had to face reality, which none of us was prepared for. Several months earlier I had begun to work in the university library. I also wrote book reviews for the newspaper *Nova Makedonija*. Ivan was teaching at the university. It was only Vlado who couldn't find work in any theatre. We didn't have as much free time to spend together. Days would go by that we didn't see each other. We no longer slept together. When we did plan to see each other, Vlado avoided us. As if he were blaming us because he was the only one having trouble getting started. When Ivan and I found ourselves alone together, we pretended nothing had changed. But we both knew it was no longer the same.

One evening we were supposed to meet at Boni to decide where to go together on vacation. That trip was supposed to bring us closer together. Vlado was the only one who thought that was impossible. Still, he finally agreed to meet with us. Ivan showed up around closing. 'Let's go to Crete,' he said.

Then, at the beginning of summer, I went to the sea for the first time. A dirt road ran from the campground where we were staying to the nearby villages. To get to the nearest store we had to walk an hour. There were other campers, too, but our tent was the farthest away. It was clear from the first days that Vlado had been right. Our lives had completely changed. It was impossible for us to live as we had when we were students. I was the only one who didn't accept our changed reality. We rarely saw Ivan. He spent most of his time with the other campers. Sometimes he didn't even come back to sleep. When he saw us in the water, he'd wave to us, but he'd keep on enjoying himself with the others. Vlado and I would go down to the beach, read books, walk to the village. Once when we went to the village to buy some food, Ivan was sitting in front of a store with a girl. They were drinking beer. He acted like he didn't see us. We went into the store without saying anything. We didn't see him for several days after that.

He turned up one evening. We were already asleep when he arrived. He lay down between us. We still had a few days until our holiday ended. I believed that many things could change in those two days. But when we woke up, he was already gone.

He didn't come back the last day either. Vlado said he wasn't planning to go looking for him. But I didn't want to return without him. I looked around all the tents. He wasn't anywhere. It was as if the sea had swallowed him up. I told Vlado to go alone if he wanted to, but I was going to stay and wait for Ivan. When I began to pack up Ivan's things, I saw that his passport wasn't there. 'He's already gone,' said Vlado. Up until the last moment I didn't want to believe it. Even when we boarded the boat and even after we had been sailing for a half hour, I thought he would appear on the deck.

We returned, just the two of us.

12.

When we got back to Skopje, we never mentioned him again. Several months later I moved in with Vlado. We began our life together. But there was always an emptiness between us. Ivan's absence always followed us. We missed him a lot. But we didn't show it. Sometimes, when one of us wanted to tell something that all three of us had done together, we always spoke as if it had just been the two of us. This wasn't the first time he had gone away. When he disappeared on the island it wasn't like the times before. We knew he wasn't going to come back. That's why we felt such bitterness.

For a long time, we tried to convince ourselves that we liked that it was just the two of us. Especially Vlado. He kept saying how happy he was to have me. And I began to love his presence. Sometimes I woke up during the night and embraced him. At those moments it was as if I wanted to convince myself that he was beside me. It filled me with a sense of security. I felt more and more that he really did love me. Everything he did was for me to feel good.

Ten years after Ivan disappeared from the island, I ran into him at the market. He hadn't changed at all. It was as if time had stood still for him. I wanted to run away, but it was too late. He was already walking towards me. Nothing could escape him. He began talking as if nothing had happened. 'Remember that girl we met on the island? Well, I married her.' I wanted to tell him that he was the one who met her, not us. 'We have a daughter too. Her name is Miriam. Like Capote's Miriam.' He took out his cell phone to show me a picture of his daughter. 'How's Vlado?' he asked. But he didn't wait for me to answer, just continued talking about himself. At one point he said, 'I have to go get Miriam from day care.' He turned to go, but then came back. 'I am so glad that you and Vlado stayed together. He always loved you.'

After that meeting, all the anger that I felt for him, I directed at Vlado. I began to criticize him for everything. Everything he did bothered me. If he threw his clothes on the chair, I threw them on the floor and told him to put them where they belonged. If he didn't clear the dishes after eating, I threw them in the garbage can. I kept finding reasons for us to argue. I would take hold of any little thing and begin shouting. He would usually say nothing. When he hugged me at night, I'd get too warm. I would push him away, or I'd go to the other room, until finally I had completely moved over into the guest room. When he got drunk and would get up on a table to recite poetry, I was ashamed of him. When someone would tell me that I must really enjoy being with him, I'd answer that as a partner he was totally boring. When the two of us were at home, we were silent most of the time, but if I said anything, it was that I couldn't stand him.

At first, he didn't understand my behaviour. He'd apologise as if he really were in the wrong. He'd promise that he would change even though he hadn't done anything. He kept begging me to tell him what had happened. But I didn't give in. 'Ask yourself,' I'd say. It was only several months later that he learned the truth. He was celebrating his birthday that evening. To please me, he had decided not to invite too many friends to dinner, just our closest ones. One of the friends, who had been Vlado's friend since they were students together, asked whether we knew that Ivan had got married. Vlado tried to change the subject, but I felt this would be an excellent opportunity to wound him.

'He has a kid too. We saw each other at the market a little while ago,' I said. After that evening, Vlado was almost never at home. And when he did come, he was drunk most of the time. He never asked me about that meeting.

13.

'When we retire, I want us to live on the island. We'll buy a house on a beach, and we'll look after the sea turtles,' said Vlado. 'The *Caretta caretta* turtles,' said Kareta. Divna Fisher and Ilinka Indira were pounding wooden stakes into the ground. 'We're going to hang gold ribbons on them to mark where the turtles have laid their eggs. From May to September the females come out onto the beach. Usually in the dark. They dig holes with their fins, and that's where they lay the eggs. It's too bad you won't be here when the young turtles begin to emerge,' said Divna Fisher.

Nita India and Mila India came with Saffron. They had with them a one-eyed dog. 'This is Voodoo Eye,' said Saffron when he saw me looking at the dog. 'Voodoo Eye was abandoned by his owners, who were only keeping him to fight with other dogs. He didn't exactly come out the best in those fights, so they got rid of him.' He pulled some sandwiches out of a bag and gave one to each of us. 'They're vegan. With pesto and almonds,' he said.

Nita India was carrying the aquarium with a picture of a turtle pasted on it. Mila India was carrying a banner, which was upside down, with 'Donate to Save the Turtles' written on it. Nita India approached Vlado with the aquarium. 'Put something in and we'll name the first turtle that comes out of its shell after you,' she said. Vlado took out some money and dropped it into the aquarium. 'Call it Ivan,' he told her.

That was the first time in twenty years he had said the name aloud.

There was no trace of bitterness in his voice. On his face was a look of relief.

All at once, the sun disappeared. It was dark everywhere. In the distance, a small turtle kept appearing and disappearing. It would poke out its head, then, frightened by the waves, it would retreat back into its shell. But it didn't give up. Clumsily and unsure of itself, it made its way to the sea. Until a wave completely washed over it.

RETURN

1.

At the beginning of summer, twenty days after leaving the hospital, I was standing by the window of a hotel room and looking at the beach. Under a beach chair was a yellow cat. Raindrops were running down its fur.

'What does it feel like to be loved?'

'It rained all night. It's still raining.'

Now the cat had thrown itself under a different beach chair, on which lay someone's forgotten scarf. All I could see from under it was its tail.

'What does it feel like after you've been unfaithful to someone?'

'We need to leave the room by noon.'

I was no longer looking at the cat. A girl with a black umbrella was calling someone.

'Is it possible, after everything, to forget the past?'

'A little while ago I saw a cat in the rain.'

I wasn't looking anymore at the cat, or the girl. I left the room, leaving the door open. On the stairs I passed an American couple. They were soaking wet. Behind them they had left traces of water. If they were lovers, they would easily be discovered. The receptionist was smoking on the terrace. 'There's nothing for you,' he said when he saw me. 'But, perhaps an umbrella… would you like an umbrella…'

The rain was stronger than it had looked from inside. My legs slipped in the sand. I pulled away the scarf. The cat was looking at me, frightened.

When I got back, the door to the room was still open. The suitcases were standing by the bed.

'Who do you want to go back with?'
I didn't say anything. I pressed the cat tightly to my chest.
'We'll all go back, all three of us,' he said.

MEN ALONE
Özgür Uyanık

978-1-914595-82-0
£10 | Paperback

'Wry, moving, and beautifully
crafted... rich and multilayered'
– Tristan Hughes

'A powerful and poetic new voice
in the art of storytelling'
– Selcuk Altun

WOMEN WHO
BLOW ON KNOTS
Ece Temelkuran
Translated from Turkish by
Alexander Dawe

978-1-914595-53-0
£10.99 | Paperback

Winner of the Edinburgh
International Book Festival First
Book Award

'A feminist, magic-realist trip
through the Arab Spring'
– *The Spectator*

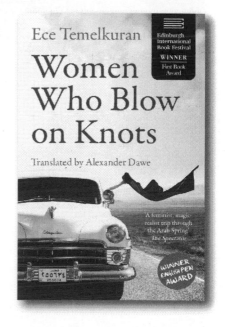

PARTHIAN TRANSLATIONS

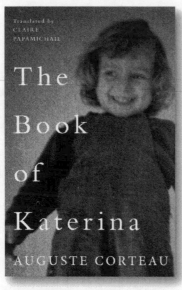

THE BOOK OF KATERINA

Auguste Corteau

Translated from Greek
by Claire Papamichail

—

£10.00
978-1-912681-26-6

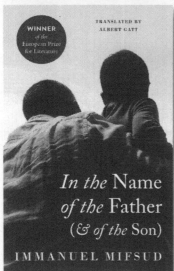

IN THE NAME OF THE FATHER (& OF THE SON)

Immanuel Mifsud

Translated from Maltese
by Albert Gatt

—

£6.99
978-1-912681-30-3

Creative Europe

PARTHIAN TRANSLATIONS

THE LAST DAY

Owain Owain

Translated from Welsh
by Emyr Humphreys

£9.00
9781914595806

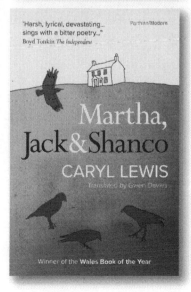

MARTHA, JACK AND SHANCO

Caryl Lewis

Winner of the Wales
Book of the Year

Translated from Welsh by Gwen Davies

£9.99
978-1-912681-77-8

Supported using public funding by

ENGLISH PEN FREEDOM TO **WRITE** FREEDOM TO **READ**

ARTS COUNCIL ENGLAND

This book has been selected to receive financial assistance from English PEN's Writers in Translation programme supported by Bloomberg and Arts Council England. English PEN exists to promote literature and its understanding, uphold writers' freedoms around the world, campaign against the persecution and imprisonment of writers for stating their views, and promote the friendly co-operation of writers and free exchange of ideas. Each year, a dedicated committee of professionals selects books that are translated into English from a wide variety of foreign languages. We award grants to UK publishers to help translate, promote, market and champion these titles. Our aim is to celebrate books of outstanding literary quality, which have a clear link to the PEN charter and promote free speech and intercultural understanding.

Writers in Translation's outstanding work and contribution to diversity in the UK literary scene was recognised by Arts Council England. English PEN was awarded a threefold increase in funding to develop its support for world writing in translation. www.englishpen.org

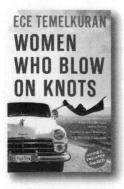